Amazing Animals of South East Asia

Cameron Macintosh

Contents

Amazing Animals of South East Asia

Where Is South East Asia?

South East Asia is a large area spanning many countries. It includes Myanmar (also called Burma), Laos, Thailand, Cambodia, Vietnam, Malaysia, Singapore, Brunei, the Philippines, Indonesia and East Timor. Some parts of South East Asia are connected to **mainland** Asia, while other parts consist of large and small islands.

A Map of South East Asia

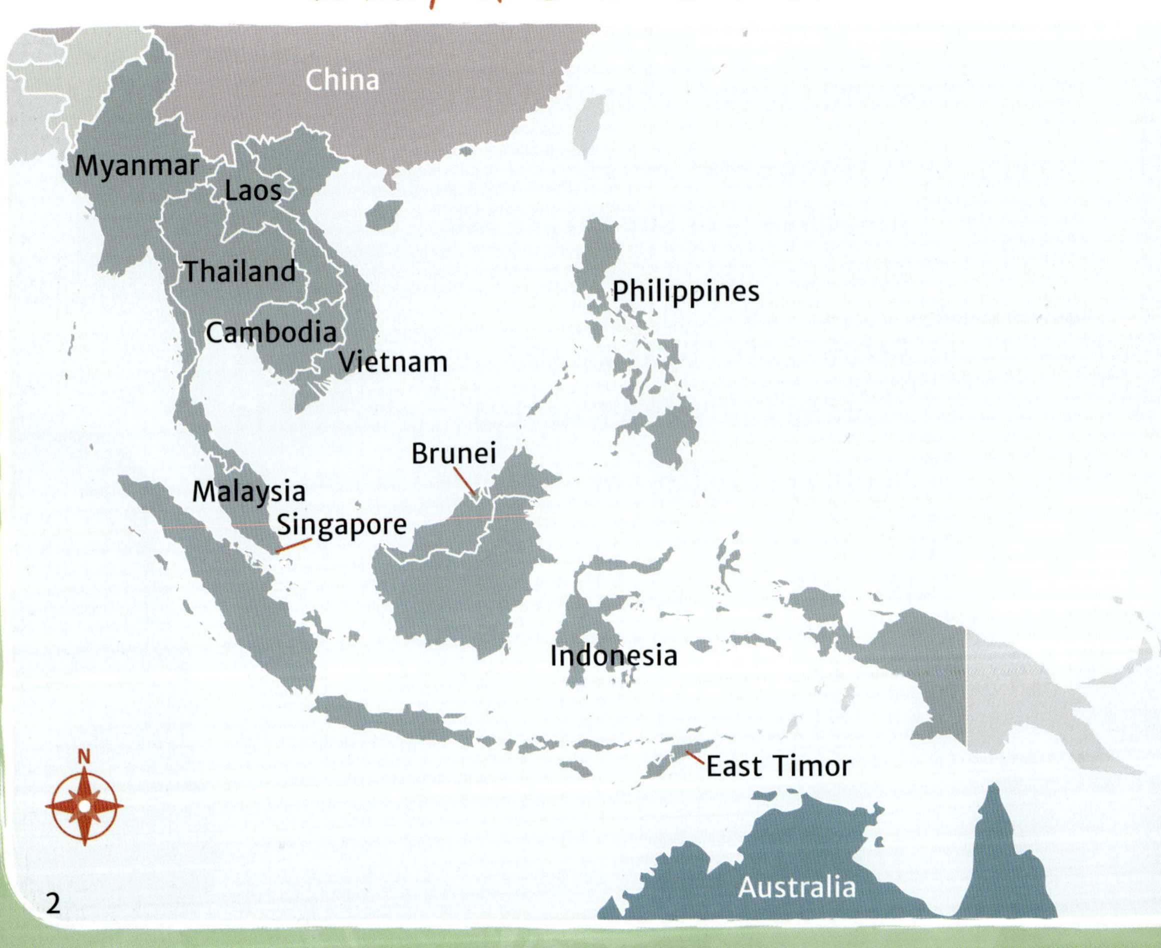

Most of South East Asia is **tropical**, so it is usually very warm and humid. In most parts of South East Asia, there are two main seasons – the dry season and the wet season.

In the dry season, there is less rain than at other times of the year, and the weather is cooler. Short, heavy rain showers occur regularly during the wet season.

The tropical rainforest in Indonesia is still green during the dry season.

Heavy rain falls during the wet season in the rainforest in Borneo.

South East Asia has a wide range of environments that vary greatly from place to place. These include mountain ranges, large areas of rainforest and extensive river systems. There are also many coral reefs near the islands and coasts of South East Asia.

Padar Island in Indonesia is unique because it has green mountains.

With so many unique environments, South East Asia provides ideal habitats for an incredibly wide range of animals. These include **amphibians**, birds, reptiles and mammals.

Great hornbills live in the tallest trees in the old rainforests.

A sun bear looks for food in a forest in Malaysia.

A gliding lizard climbs a tree in Indonesia.

Amphibians of South East Asia

More than 800 **species** of frogs and other amphibians live in the swamps and forests of South East Asia. Some species of frogs can jump surprisingly long distances to move from tree to tree, and some can even glide through the air!

Abah River Flying Frog

The Abah River flying frog is found in the forests of Indonesia, Thailand and Malaysia. It is a large green and yellow frog with a white underbelly. It spends most of its life high in the forest trees.

An Abah River flying frog sits on a branch.

The Abah River flying frog has unusually long webbed fingers and toes, and fringes of skin on its sides that allow it to glide from tree to tree.

It uses its webbing and fringes of skin like a parachute. This slows the frog's fall and gives it control over where it lands. The frog can glide through the air to catch prey such as insects, or to avoid predators such as tree snakes.

The Abah River flying frog spreads its fingers and toes to glide through the air.

Birds of South East Asia

South East Asia is home to about 2500 species of birds. At least 800 of these species are not seen in any other part of the world.

Great Hornbill

The great hornbill is a large bird found throughout South East Asia. An adult great hornbill has a black and white body and a mostly yellow **casque** (pronounced *kask*) on its bill. Its casque shows other hornbills that it is old enough to find a mate and produce offspring.

A great hornbill can use the casque on its bill to make loud noises.

When great hornbills find a mate, they usually stay together for life. Before the female great hornbill lays any eggs, she builds a barrier to seal herself inside a tree hollow. She stays there until the eggs hatch. Both parents feed the chicks through a hole in the barrier until the chicks are big enough to leave the hollow, too.

The great hornbill mainly feeds on fruit, but it also eats insects and animals such as lizards, mice and small birds.

A male great hornbill feeds fruit to a female while she lays her eggs.

Blue-tailed Bee-eater

The blue-tailed bee-eater is a colourful, lean bird with a black beak and a black stripe over its eye. It has feathers of blue, green, red and yellow. It is found throughout South East Asia, usually near rivers, lakes and wetlands.

The blue-tailed bee-eater mainly eats flying insects, particularly bees, wasps, hornets and dragonflies. It can catch these insects in mid-air!

A blue-tailed bee-eater can catch insects to eat as it flies.

Blue-tailed bee-eaters dig tunnels in soft sand.

The female blue-tailed bee-eater lays between five to seven eggs each year. Both parents take care of the eggs and look after their chicks until they are old enough to leave the nest. Blue-tailed bee-eaters that live near the sea often dig deep tunnels in the sand to lay their eggs.

Blue-tailed bee-eaters like to build their nests in large groups.

Reptiles of South East Asia

South East Asia is home to a wide range of reptiles, from small lizards to huge crocodiles. Some of these reptiles have unusual skills, such as the ability to glide through the air.

Sumatran Gliding Lizard

The Sumatran gliding lizard is a small lizard that lives in the forest of Sumatra, an island in Indonesia. It is also found in Malaysia, Singapore and the islands of Palawan in the Philippines.

The lizard has stripy patterns of grey and dark brown that make it difficult to see on tree trunks. This helps it to stay safe from predators.

The Sumatran gliding lizard can glide through the trees, using long skin flaps on the sides of its body that open out like a parachute. It uses this ability to escape from predators, or to move from tree to tree to find food, such as ants and other insects.

A gliding lizard, photographed from below, uses its skin flaps to glide.

The stripy patterns on the Sumatran gliding lizard are excellent camouflage.

Siamese Crocodile

The Siamese crocodile is a medium-sized crocodile found in freshwater rivers, lakes and swamps in Indonesia, Malaysia, Thailand, Cambodia and Vietnam. Male Siamese crocodiles can grow up to 4 metres in length, while females can grow to about 3 metres.

The Siamese crocodile is usually coloured olive green, but some can have darker green colouring. This crocodile also has a bony **crest** behind each eye.

The bony crests behind Siamese crocodiles' eyes make it different from other crocodiles.

A Siamese crocodile warms itself in the sun by a river in Thailand.

The Siamese crocodile mainly eats frogs, fish and snakes. It can feed on larger animals, too, but is not usually dangerous to humans.

The female Siamese crocodile uses mud and plants to make a nest on land. She lays her eggs in the nest in April or May, during the wet season. When the eggs hatch, she carries her young to the water in her mouth.

Mammals of South East Asia

A wide range of mammals live in South East Asia, such as elephants, bears, big cats and **primates**, such as orangutans.

Sun Bear

The sun bear is an **omnivore** that lives in the tropical rainforests of South East Asia, mostly in Malaysia. It is also found in Cambodia and on the islands of Sumatra and Borneo in Indonesia.

A sun bear walks through the rainforest.

The sun bear is the world's smallest species of bear. It gets its name from the U-shaped yellow patch on its chest, which reminds some people of the sun.

The sun bear only grows to about 1 metre tall, but it is a good climber, spending much of its time in trees. It eats a wide range of foods, including fruit, honey, beetles and ants.

The sun bear has a big yellow patch on its chest.

Sun bears can climb trees to find insects to eat.

Slow Loris

The slow loris is a nocturnal mammal found in forests and scrub in South East Asia. It gets its name from its slow movement as it climbs along tree branches with its hands and feet.

When it eats, the slow loris hangs upside-down from trees by its feet and uses its hands to hold its food. It eats fruit and plants, as well as small animals, which it hunts for at night. The slow loris has big, round eyes which help it to see well in the dark.

The slow loris uses its strong hands and feet to hang on to trees.

Despite its slow movement, the slow loris is very capable of defending itself. It produces **venom** on the insides of its elbows, which it can mix with saliva from its mouth to give a dangerous bite.

Female slow lorises even put the venom on their babies' fur to protect them from predators.

A female slow loris protects her baby at night.

Silver-backed Chevrotain

The silver-backed chevrotain (pronounced *shev-ruh-tain*) is a hooved mammal also known as a mouse-deer. It is found in the lowland forests of southern Vietnam. It looks like a deer with short legs, and only grows to the size of a small cat. The first part of its name comes from the line of silver fur on its back.

The chevrotain mostly feeds on plants, but it occasionally eats insects or other small animals, such as crabs or fish.

The silver-backed chevrotain lives in the forests of Vietnam.

This photo of a silver-backed chevrotain was taken with a hidden camera.

The silver-backed chevrotain has four parts to its stomach. These help it to digest the tough leaves and grasses that it eats. Like a cow, it **regurgitates** a **cud** from the first part of its stomach and makes it soft by chewing it. It then swallows the cud again and digests it in the other three parts.

The silver-backed chevrotain was thought to be extinct for 30 years, but it was filmed on a hidden camera in Vietnam in 2019. Scientists do not know how many chevrotains remain in the wild.

Sunda Pangolin

The Sunda pangolin is a scale-covered mammal found in the forests of South East Asia. It is mostly nocturnal, going out to hunt for ants and termites at night.

The Sunda pangolin has poor eyesight, but its strong sense of smell helps it to find food. With its powerful claws, it can dig into ant nests and termite mounds.

A Sunda pangolin uses its tail for balance.

A Sunda pangolin uses its long tongue to eat as many ants and termites as it can.

Using its 40-centimetre tongue, the Sunda pangolin can eat thousands of ants and termites in one meal.

The Sunda pangolin has a strong tail, which it can lash about to keep predators away. It can also protect itself by curling into a ball and using its sharp-edged scales as armour.

A Sunda pangolin curls into a ball for protection.

South East Asian Animals Under Threat

Many South East Asian animals face long-term challenges to their survival.

One of their biggest threats is **deforestation**. When trees and plants are cut down or removed, animals have fewer safe places to live, and face more competition for food from other animals.

Deforestation is a problem for many animals in South East Asia.

Another major problem for many animals is **poaching**. South East Asian animals, including the sun bear and the Sunda pangolin, have been hunted by humans for their meat or skins. Other animals, such as the slow loris, have been taken from the wild and sold as pets, even though they don't adjust well to **captivity**.

The most serious problem facing the animals of South East Asia is **climate change.** As Earth heats up, trees and plants that animals need for food and shelter are dying because they cannot **adapt** to higher temperatures.

South East Asia is home to many unique animals, found nowhere else on Earth. We need to do everything we can to make sure they have the very best chance of surviving into the future.

Our Search for the Silver-backed Chevrotain

By Liam Zullo, Class 4B

Day 1, 13 August

This morning, Dad and I landed at the airport in Nha Trang, southern Vietnam. We have come to Vietnam because Dad is a **zoologist**. He really wants to spot a silver-backed chevrotain in the wild, or at least get a photo of one with a hidden camera!

I'd love to see a silver-backed chevrotain, too! The chevrotain is a very rare animal, only found in a few areas in southern Vietnam.

This afternoon, we set up camp at the edge of the Hon Ba Nature Reserve. Then, we went for our first walk in search of the chevrotain. Dad's friend Nam came with us. Nam works at the university in the city of Nha Trang and studies wildlife, too.

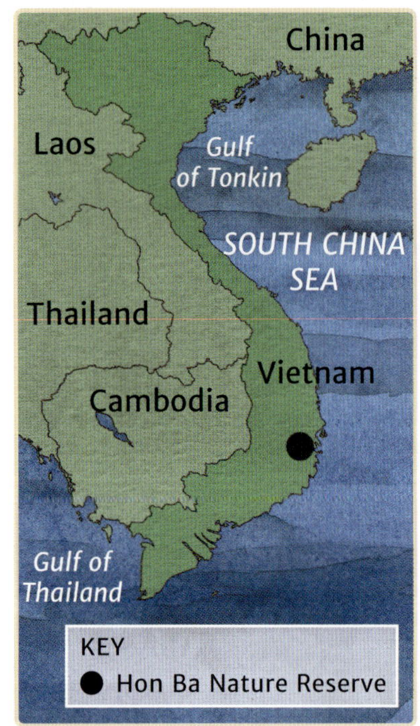

We saw all sorts of birds and bugs, and even a lemur, but there was no sign of a silver-backed chevrotain. That didn't worry us because Dad had brought his camera along. He planned to hide his camera and take some photos without the animals knowing. After walking for about twenty minutes, we placed the camera in front of a tree, facing a leafy shrub that Nam said chevrotains might like to eat.

Dad set up the camera so that it would only take photos if an animal moved in front of it. We covered it in camouflage cloth, and I found some leaves and branches to hide it. Although silver-backed chevrotains mostly come out in the daytime, Dad planned to leave the camera turned on all night ... just in case.

By then, we were all quite tired, so we hiked back to camp and went to bed straight after dinner.

Day 2, 14 August

As soon as we woke up this morning, we had breakfast and hurried into the forest with Nam to check the camera. We looked at last night's photos. There was a clear photo of a moth, as well as one of a mouse, but no photo of a chevrotain.

"Don't worry," said Dad. "We still have another two days here. I think we'll have better luck if we move the camera deeper into the forest."

We hiked further into the reserve. On our way, we saw some droppings that Dad and Nam thought could have been left by a chevrotain!

We set up the camera beneath some shrubs and spent the rest of the day exploring the forest. We didn't see any chevrotains, but I did spot a pangolin and some beautiful birds!

Day 3, 15 August

This morning, we trekked back through the forest to check the camera again. There wasn't much more to look at when Dad showed us the screen – just photos of a bird and a frog!

"We only have one more night," I said. "I don't think we're going to see a chevrotain."

"I don't think so either," Dad said to me, "but at least we've had fun trying."

Day 4, 16 August

This morning, Dad said, "Come on, Liam, it's time to go back into the forest to pack up the camera."

Dad didn't say much as we trekked with Nam through the forest. I knew Dad was feeling disappointed.

An hour later, we arrived back where we had left the camera. Dad picked it up and pressed a button on its side. Suddenly, his face glowed with excitement, and he showed us the screen. At 4.09 yesterday afternoon, a silver-backed chevrotain had sniffed at the camera!

"This is incredible!" I said to Dad. "We didn't see a chevrotain with our own eyes, but this photo is definitely the next best thing!"

Glossary

adapt (*verb*)	to adjust to different conditions
amphibians (*noun*)	animals that live part of their lives in water and on land
captivity (*noun*)	the keeping of animals as pets or locked in enclosures
casque (*noun*)	a horn or helmet on a bird's bill, usually made of bone
climate change (*noun*)	a change in weather patterns around the world
crest (*noun*)	a raised area on an animal's head
cud (*noun*)	already swallowed food that an animal brings back up into its mouth to chew
deforestation (*noun*)	when trees in a forest are cut down to clear land for other uses
mainland (*noun*)	the main part of a continent rather than its islands
omnivore (*noun*)	an animal that can eat both plants and other animals
poaching (*noun*)	illegally killing or catching an animal
primates (*noun*)	mammals such as monkeys, apes and humans with forward-facing eyes and long fingers

regurgitates (*verb*) brings up food that has already been swallowed

species (*noun*) particular types of animals

tropical (*adjective*) very hot but not dry; often rainy or humid

venom (*noun*) a poisonous substance produced by an animal

zoologist (*noun*) a type of scientist that studies animals

Index